KU-360-341

TEARS
of a Friend

Jo Cotterill

Ransom

SHADES 2.0
Tears of a Friend
by Jo Cotterill

Published by Ransom Publishing Ltd.
Radley House, 8 St. Cross Road, Winchester, Hampshire SO23 9HX, UK
www.ransom.co.uk

ISBN   978 178127 212 1
First published in 2004
This updated edition published by Ransom Publishing 2013

CONTENTS

One   7

Two   12

Three   17

Four   20

Five   26

Six   31

Seven   37

Eight   40

Nine   46

Ten   51

ONE

'It's just not fair,' says my best friend Claire.
'Parents are so mean. Midnight isn't late. I
mean, not *really*.'

I look at her. Claire is fourteen, the same
age as me. But, unlike me, she's pretty. No,
not pretty. *Gorgeous*. She has this long,
blonde hair. It's silky and shiny, like in the
adverts. Mine is frizzy and always looks a

mess.

She flicks her hair while she talks. It makes her look like a model and boys love it. I tried to flick mine once, too. Mum thought I had nits.

'You're not listening, Cassie!' says Claire. 'They've grounded me for *two weeks*!'

'But didn't they say you had to be in by eleven?' I ask.

'Whose side are you on?' Claire snaps. 'You know I had to go to Nick's gig.' (Nick is her older brother. I fancy him rotten, but I wouldn't ever admit it. Even under torture.)

'Was it good?' I ask.

'Brilliant. There was this fit bloke there – '

I knew it. I bet she snogged him.

The school bell rings. We pick up our bags.

'Oh, by the way, did you know Louise is having a party?' says Claire.

Suddenly I feel very excited. 'Really? When?'

'Next Thursday.'

'Thursday?' I am surprised. 'Who has a party on a school night?'

Claire shrugs. 'I dunno. It's a sort of *well done* party for her sister.'

'What for?'

'She passed her driving test at last.'

We grin at each other. We don't like Louise's sister. We found it very funny when she failed three times. Ha ha ha!

'But will your parents let you go?' I ask.

'Who cares? I'm going anyway. I'm fed up with being treated like a child. Can't wait 'til I'm sixteen.'

'Me too.'

'They won't be able to boss me around then.'

By this time we are sitting down in class.

It's maths with Mr Price. We laugh at him a lot. When he gets embarrassed the back of his neck goes red. Our class embarrasses him a lot on purpose. We sent him a valentine's card from the geography teacher. We knew he fancied her. His neck stayed red for forty-five minutes. I know because I timed it.

When the bell goes, Claire says to me 'God, maths is boring, isn't it?'

'God, yeah,' I say. Actually I quite like maths. But of course I can't say that.

'I was thinking about Louise's party,' says Claire. She sighs. I know what's coming. 'I've got nothing to wear.'

We always go through this. Claire's wardrobe is twice the size of mine. She has loads of really nice shoes too. I counted mine the other day.

I have:

Two pairs of trainers

Three pairs of sandals (two with sand in, one that gives me blisters)

One pair of 'smart' shoes for school

One pair of 'cool' shoes with heels

Oh, and one pair of wellies.

I have also grown out of my one decent dress. Not upwards, just outwards.

'I've got nothing to wear either,' I say.

Claire cheers up. 'Let's go shopping!'

'Okay. How about two o'clock tomorrow?'

TWO

Next day is Saturday. There's a new shopping centre near me. It's got Topshop and Miss Selfridge and all the cheap places like Primark and Matalan. We've been coming here since it opened a few months ago and I always spend all my money. Not that I get much.

It's busy as usual. The centre is always

packed on a Saturday.

'Over here, Cassie!' calls Claire. She looks stunning. Pink crop-top and tight jeans. And –

'Oh my God!' I gasp. 'Have you had your belly-button pierced?'

'Fooled you!' giggles Claire. She shows me the little sparkly jewel. 'It's stick-on. I bought it just now.'

'It looks really cool,' I say. Now I want one too. But that would be copying. And my tummy isn't flat like hers. It would look silly on me.

'Come on, there's some new stuff in H&M.' Claire drags me off.

We have a brilliant time. I love trying on clothes. Dresses, trousers, little tops, big baggy jumpers, short skirts – it's how I imagine heaven to be. One big shopping centre in the sky, where you can shop forever.

We're in New Look. Claire has got this dress on that looks amazing. (Of course. I mean, she could wear a dustbin sack and look amazing.)

I'm pulling on a dark-green velvet top. I gasp at myself in the mirror. I look *fantastic*. The top is very low cut. I have a cleavage!

I turn to Claire. 'What do you think?'

'Hang on a minute,' she says. 'Do you think this makes me look fat?'

'No,' I say, 'but look at me!'

She glances at me. 'It's all right.'

She's looking at herself again.

I'm suddenly angry. 'Look properly!' I say loudly.

Claire looks surprised. And a bit annoyed. But she *does* look at me. 'Yeah, it's nice. Bit revealing though, isn't it? For you, I mean.'

'What do you mean, for me?'

14

I can feel hot, red anger boiling up inside me.

'Well,' Claire says with a shrug, 'it's just not your style.'

I am really mad now.

'And what exactly is my style? Looking *boring*, I suppose? So that *you* look better when you stand next to me. Like I'm your shadow or something. Like I don't matter – it's all about *you*! Well thanks a lot!'

As I pull the green top over my head I hear something rip. I don't care.

'See you around, Claire,' I say. She looks really silly, her mouth hanging open as she stares at me. I storm out of the changing room. I fling the top at the shop assistant.

'No thanks,' I say. 'It's not my *style*.'

What an exit!

I am very impressed with myself. To start with. But after about five minutes I begin to feel really down. When I get home I burst into tears. I'm angry with myself and with Claire. After a while I'm not angry any more, just sad.

Maybe I can make it up with Claire tomorrow? But why should I? She should say sorry first.

I fall asleep with a headache.

THREE

Monday at school is a nightmare. I haven't seen or heard from Claire since Saturday. Mr Price tries to make us work together on a problem.

'I don't want to work with Cassie today,' says Claire. She won't look at me.

'All right then,' says Mr Price. I can tell he's surprised.

I pretend not to mind, but something inside hurts.

At break-times I have no one to talk to. Claire and I hang around all the time together. I've never needed any other friends. Now I wish I'd made the effort.

Every time Claire walks past me, she flicks her hair and looks away. I kind of hope she will come up to me. Say she is sorry and can we be friends again? But she doesn't, and I can't do it myself.

Over the next few days it's like we were never friends at all. Like our history together never happened. I make friends with Isabel, the nerdy girl in the class. She's so grateful someone has finally talked to her. It makes me feel sorry for her. She has even less confidence than I do. It annoys me in a way. I wish she'd stand up for herself a bit.

Is this how Claire thinks of me?

Even Mum notices something odd.

'Where's Claire these days?' she says. 'I haven't seen her for ages.'

'We're not friends any more,' I say.

She doesn't ask again.

The day before the party, I decide something. Maybe it's time to make some changes. Maybe Claire's right, in a way. I should make more of an effort with myself, the way I look. Maybe then I'd have more confidence, be more popular.

I go back to New Look and buy the green velvet top. The one with the rip in it is still on the rail. I choose a different one, hoping the shop assistants don't recognise me.

Watch out, world! The new, improved Cassie is here!

FOUR

On the night of the party I should feel excited. Instead, I just feel nervous and sick. Normally Claire and I would get ready for a party together. We would spend hours making ourselves look awesome. Well, she would look awesome. I would look sort of OK.

I nearly decide not to go. But then I feel angry. Why should Claire stop me having a good time? Most of the people I know from school will be there. I can have a good time without her.

And her gorgeous brother Nick might be there too …

I pull on the dark-green velvet top. I'm right, it does make me look amazing. I decide to wear a short, black skirt and my heeled shoes. I wish I had knee-length boots, but I've spent my allowance for this month. Again.

I spend ages on my make-up. I'm not very good at it yet. We're not allowed to wear it at school. I practise at weekends, but I still haven't got the hang of eye-shadow. I often put too much on and look like I've got two black eyes.

There's not much I can do with my hair. Whatever style I try, it always ends up looking a frizzy mess. I put loads of hair gel in it. It does look quite nice but it feels horrible, like stiff glue.

I'm finally ready.

'You look nice,' says my mum.

'Thanks.' I wonder if she means it. She doesn't like me wearing short skirts. Maybe she's just being kind.

'Honestly, who has a party on a school night?' she says, shaking her head. 'Why couldn't it be tomorrow? None of you will be in a fit state for school in the morning.'

I mumble something and open the front door.

'Hang on, I'll walk you to the party,' calls Mum, pulling a coat on.

Horror!

'No, Mum! Honestly, I'll be fine,' I say quickly.

How embarrassing – what if anyone sees me?

'Look, I'm not letting you walk in the dark all the way there,' she says. 'I'll walk you to the corner, OK?'

'Mum … '

'It's not up for discussion, Cassie. Here, put your coat on.' She holds it out.

'No thanks, I'll be fine.'

'It's cold out.'

She's right, but there's no way I'm wearing my school coat to the party.

'Don't nag, Mum.'

She frowns. 'All right, freeze to death. See if I care.'

We set off. Within five seconds I have goose-pimples. But I can't rub my arms to keep warm. Mum will say, 'I told you so.'

At the corner of Louise's road, she stops. 'Have a good time then, snowman.'

'Thanks,' I say through chattering teeth. My feet are starting to hurt, too. The shoes rub my heels.

'No later than eleven,' she says. 'And get someone to walk you home, or call me.'

'Yes, Mum.'

I leave her at the corner. I know she'll watch me until I reach Louise's house. It annoys me a bit, but I'm also secretly glad.

As I reach Louise's front door, I hear a shout to my right.

'Hey, Cassie!' It's Isabel. I almost die of shame. I didn't realise she was coming. We haven't talked about it. I didn't think it would be her sort of thing.

But here she is, tottering along in four-inch heels. She looks ridiculous. She's wearing a sort of fishnet top over a black vest. Her hair is back-combed and piled on top of her head. And she's even worse than me at make-up.

But it means I've got to go into the party

with her. People will think that we came together.

Oh well. Better get it over with. I give her a weak smile. Then I ring the door bell.

FIVE

It's not Louise who opens the door. It's some boy I don't know.

'Hi,' he says. His eyes are kind of red. 'Come in.'

Isabel and I step into the hall. There's loud music coming from the front room, but there's a huge crowd of people in the way. I shrink back against the wall.

'Come on!' calls Isabel. 'The fun's always in the kitchen!' She bounces off, pushing her way through the crush. I stay where I am.

There are a lot of people here I don't know. Louise's sister must have invited them. Most of them seem a lot older than me.

Then my heart stops. It's Nick, Claire's brother. He's wearing a leather jacket and holding a cigarette. He looks *amazing*.

'Hi,' I blurt out, before my brain can stop my mouth. 'I'm Cassie, Claire's friend.'

Nick turns to look at me, and then – I can't believe this – *I put my hand out*. Like I want to shake hands with him! How stupid is that?

'Oh yeah, hi,' he says, although I can tell he doesn't recognise me. He ignores my hand and I snatch it back quickly.

'How are you?' I burble. 'I hear your gig went really well last week.'

Nick stares at me.

'Yeah, it was cool.' He takes a swig from a beer bottle. His eyes slide down. 'Nice top,' he says. Then he pushes past me and goes into the front room.

I reach to my neckline to try to pull it up a bit higher. I should feel pleased that he liked my top, but weirdly I feel a bit dirty. I didn't like the way he looked at me, as though he could see right through my clothes. And I'm cursing myself for being so stupid. I mean, going to shake hands! My face burns with shame, and I head towards the kitchen, avoiding people's eyes.

'Sorry,' I say as I push past a couple snogging by the stairs.

'Watch where you're going,' snaps the girl. It's Claire. Her eyes open wide when she sees me. But then she pulls the boy's head towards her and starts kissing him again. It's not someone I know. I go past, feeling sick.

The kitchen is buzzing. There's a funny smell in the air too, like Mum's musk perfume. I pour myself a Coke and try not to catch anyone's eye. This is worse than I thought. Why did I come?

'Hiya, sexy.' A boy with floppy, dark hair nudges me with his hip. He looks about eighteen and his eyes are fixed on my boobs. I begin to wonder whether the top was a mistake. 'Want to have a bit of fun?' He dangles a little bag in front of my eyes. It looks like it's full of dried leaves. I frown.

'What's that?'

The boy grins. His blue eyes look really huge.

'It's heaven in a bag, baby.'

Then it hits me. He's offering me drugs.

'No thank you,' I squeak out. My face must show how horrified I am.

'Ah, go on. You look like the kind of girl who needs to relax.'

He's very tall and leans over me. I shrink back against the fridge. 'No,' I say, but my mouth has gone dry. His gaze drops again to my cleavage and he reaches out a hand. I don't know why, but I'm completely frozen. My mind is saying *move, move!* But my body isn't listening. His eyes are hypnotising.

'Hiya, Cassie,' says a cheerful voice from behind the boy. 'Fancy some fresh air?' And a hand reaches round and firmly grasps my wrist.

SIX

It's not until we're out of the kitchen that I start to breathe. I don't even know who's rescued me, until he turns around and grins at me. White teeth in a dark face.

'Mark!' He's in my class at school, but I don't know him that well.

'You looked a bit desperate,' he says, letting go of my wrist. He grins at me.

'Hope I did the right thing.'

'Yeah, thanks,' I say, my head spinning. My body is just waking up and it's feeling a bit wobbly.

'You don't have to go outside with me. It was just to get you away from that bloke.' Mark has to raise his voice as we head into the hall.

'No, I'd like to,' I yell. 'It's too hot in here.'

As we head out the front door, we pass a couple going up the stairs.

'Isn't that your friend Claire?' Mark says suddenly.

I turn. Claire is heading up the stairs, giggling. The guy she was snogging earlier is grabbing her bum as he follows her. Her skirt is practically up around her waist. My jaw drops.

'Somebody's got lucky then,' says Mark with a grin.

I follow Mark out into the front garden. The noise level drops, and I find myself taking big gulps of the cold air. Then I shiver. I wish I'd brought my coat now!

'Are you all right?' Mark looks at me in concern.

'Cold,' I explain. 'My mum told me to bring my coat and I didn't.'

'Hang on,' says Mark, and goes back into the house. When he comes out, he's carrying a big winter coat.

'Where did you get that?' I ask.

He shrugs. 'It was hanging by the front door. Put it on.'

'It's not mine!'

'So? No one will miss it for a few minutes, will they? You can put it back afterwards.'

I hesitate for a moment, then give in. 'All right. Won't you be cold?'

Mark grins and holds up a big fleece.

'Borrowed this one too.'

I laugh. 'You!' It is such a relief to put on the coat! It's thick, and soon I'm much warmer. 'Thanks.'

'No problem.'

Mark sits down next to me and there's a bit of an awkward pause. I'm really grateful to Mark for helping me out. But I'm also beginning to wonder if he wants something in return. Is he going to try to kiss me? I sneak a sideways look at him. He's nice, I guess, but I don't really fancy him. Does he fancy me? What if he kisses me and I don't like it? Should I let him kiss me because he brought me the coat? My head hurts.

'I hate parties,' Mark says suddenly.

'What?'

'Parties. I hate them. Everyone gets dressed up in completely stupid clothes. Everyone tries to drink too much to show that they're really cool. Then you're expected to get off with someone you don't even like. And probably throw up. And that's what people think is having a "good time"! It stinks.'

'I know exactly what you mean!' I say in relief. 'What's so cool about being ill all night?'

'Or getting slobbered over.'

'Or having to use the bathroom when there's no toilet paper.'

'Or someone spilling beer all over you.'

We grin at each other.

'Why did we come?' Mark says.

'Because – ' I start. 'I don't know.'

'I like being out here, though,' he says.

'Me too.' And I mean it.

He produces a bottle of lemonade from behind his back. 'Want a really uncool drink?'

I smile. 'Definitely.'

SEVEN

After that, we get chatting really easily. It's nice, actually. I don't have any friends that are boys (mostly because they're all really stupid), but Mark's OK. And once I've realised that he's not about to grope me, or try to snog me, we get on surprisingly well. We talk about school, friends, family. I tell him about my row with Claire and he listens.

It must be about half an hour later when there's a load of noise at the front door. Some girl comes running out. Her face is all streaked with mascara and lipstick and she's got no shoes on.

It's Claire. She nearly trips on the paving slabs and I find myself going to help her.

'Claire, what's the matter?'

She stares at me like she's never seen me before. 'Get off me, get off me!' she screams. She pulls away and stumbles into the road.

I follow her. 'Claire, are you OK?' Of course she's not OK, she looks awful. 'What's happened?' But she ignores me and runs off down the road in her tights. 'What should we do?' I turn to Mark.

'Nothing,' he says, staring after Claire. 'You can't help someone who doesn't want to be helped. Does she live nearby?'

'Yeah, the next street.'

'Then she'll be home in a minute. She'll be all right.'

Thinking of Claire's wide, staring eyes and tear-stained face, I'm not so sure.

EIGHT

It's only ten o'clock and Mum's surprised
that I'm home so early. She likes the look of
Mark though, I can tell.

'Thanks so much for walking her home,'
she says, giving him a warm smile. 'You're
in Cassie's class, is that right?'

I have to practically push him out of the
front door to prevent Mum asking him in

for a coffee. I mean, talking to Mark on my own is one thing. I'm not sure I want my Mum asking him questions about what his parents do, where he lives, all that. I think Mark understands. He gives me a wink as he goes.

'See you tomorrow, Cassie.'

'Yeah.' I give a bit of a grin, as if to say *aren't parents embarrassing?*

'You didn't have to be so rude,' Mum complains. 'I was going to ask him in for coffee.'

See? I knew it.

I make some excuse about being really tired and head off to my room. But it takes me ages to get to sleep. I keep thinking about Claire, going upstairs with that boy and running out of the party in tears. I really hope she got home all right. I text her, but get no reply.

She's not at school for registration the next day. Or break. Or lunch. I'm so worried about her I can't concentrate on anything. Mark tries to talk to me in French, but I'm so busy thinking about Claire I don't even hear him, and he gets told off. I get yelled at by teachers all day, and Mr Price gives me detention. By the end of the day, I've sent her sixteen texts and had nothing back.

When the detention is finally over, I decide there's only one thing to do. I don't go home; instead I go straight round to Claire's house.

Claire's dad opens the door. He works from home.

'Hi, Cassie. We haven't seen you for a while. Have you come to see Claire?' He frowns. 'I hope you can be a good influence on her. We caught her coming back from a party last night. She was supposed to be grounded.' He sighs.

'Oh,' I say blankly.

'I don't know what we're going to do. She just doesn't listen to us anymore.'

She's probably just going through a phase,' I say, repeating what my mum has said a thousand times about me.

He nods. 'I guess so.' Then he seems to remember why I'm here and steps back from the door. 'Go on up. She's just got home from school.'

I glance at him, surprised, but decide not to say anything. He obviously doesn't know that Claire wasn't in school today. I make my way up the blue-carpeted stairs.

I hesitate outside Claire's door. She's got her 'Do Not Disturb' sign on the handle. We made them in D&T at school. What if she doesn't want to see me? But I can't stand outside her door all afternoon, so I knock and go in.

'Claire? It's me.'

Claire is lying on her bed, in her school uniform, all curled up. She's got her back to the door.

'I knew it was you,' she says in a muffled voice. 'I'm surprised Dad let you in, seeing as he's in a right mood with me.' She doesn't turn round, so I carefully sit on the side of the bed.

'Are you OK?' I ask. 'Only you weren't in school today … '

She sits up at this.

'Ssh, not so loud. I wanted to stay home but Dad would have pestered me all day, so I pretended to go out as usual.'

'Where did you go?' I ask.

'What do you care?' She glares at me. 'I thought you were fed up with being my shadow?'

'I was,' I say hotly. 'But I was worried about you.' I feel really cross with her. I've come all this way to see her (well, all right, a few minutes out of my way) and she's acting like a drama queen. I stand up. 'But I can see it was a waste of time. See you around.' I turn to go.

'No, Cassie, wait!' Claire reaches out a hand. 'Don't go, Cass. I need to talk to someone. Please.'

I look at her. 'Go on then. What happened at the party?'

She takes a deep breath. 'That boy – he tried to – you know, Cass. He tried to make me have sex with him.'

NINE

I guess my face must show what I'm feeling, because she quickly says, 'I'm all right. Really. It didn't happen.'

I sit down on the bed again. 'You'd better start from the beginning.'

'Well, you saw me with that guy by the stairs,' Claire says. I nod. 'I met him about an hour before you showed up. He seemed really nice, said he went to school with Louise's sister. In Year Thirteen. Anyway, he seemed to really like me, and I didn't have anyone to talk to. I mean, normally I'd have talked to you … ' She trails off. 'I'm sorry, about before.'

'It doesn't matter,' I say. 'Go on.'

'Well, I couldn't believe that he was really interested in me. I mean, he was nearly eighteen, and he was so fit! He could have had anyone! I told him I was sixteen.'

'Claire!'

She looks sheepish. 'I know, but I thought he wouldn't be interested if he knew the truth. Anyway, he started kissing me, and it was really nice. I was a bit nervous to start with but I got the hang of it. And he kept getting me drinks, which helped. I think he put something in the Coke, because I was laughing at everything. And then he said, "Do you want a tour of the house?" and I just giggled like it was the funniest thing ever.'

I groan.

'I know, I know.' Claire bites her lip. 'I was such an idiot! Anyway, he took me upstairs.' She stops and takes a deep breath. 'It wasn't a tour, of course, he took me straight into a bedroom. But I didn't notice at the time, because he was still kissing me and telling me I was gorgeous. Then I sort of tripped over, and we both fell on the bed. I was laughing so much I didn't think much of it, but then he started touching me. Putting his hands up my skirt and stuff.' She shudders.

'What did you do?'

Claire looks at me, her eyes big and swimmy.

'I didn't know *what* to do. I just sort of lay

there for a bit, trying to move his hands away. And then I thought, maybe I should let him – you know – because I *had* been snogging him. And I did like him, sort of. Maybe I'd been leading him on. I shouldn't have snogged him in the first place. I should have said no right at the beginning, not halfway through.'

I shake my head.

'No, no, you can say *no* at any point. That's what my mum always says.'

'But when he realised I wasn't going to let him,' says Claire, a tear falling down her cheek, 'he got really mad. He said I owed him, that he couldn't stop now. Once boys got started they couldn't stop.'

I stare in horror. 'That's not true, is it?'

'I don't know. I just kept pushing him away, but he was so much stronger, Cassie, he was holding me down. I couldn't do anything. I was struggling and I think I was yelling, but it's all a bit of a blur. I thought I was losing, Cass, I was getting really tired fighting him off. And then – ' Claire gulps and takes a sobbing breath. 'Then Louise came in.'

TEN

'*Louise?*' I say in amazement.

'Yeah,' Claire smiles shakily. 'She went ballistic. Turns out we were in her parents' room. She was yelling about us being disgusting and didn't we have any respect.'

I let out a giggle. I can't help it.

'What did the boy say?'

'I don't know,' Claire says. 'He was trying

to find his trousers.'

I start giggling properly.

'His trousers?'

'Yeah. I just grabbed my bag and ran out.' Claire grins. 'Last I saw, Louise was whacking him over the head with her mum's box of tissues.'

We look at each other and burst out laughing. We laugh and laugh and roll on the bed, clutching our sides.

Claire's dad pops his head in to see what all the noise is about.

'Good,' he says, smiling. 'Glad to see you two have made up.'

We laugh even more at this. Who would have thought such a horrible event could make us friends again? I'm picturing Louise whacking some seventeen-year-old with a tissue box, and Claire is just laughing because she can't stop.

In the end, we calm down, just letting out the occasional giggle. We lie on the bed together and look up at the ceiling.

'Are you going to tell anyone?' I ask.

'Like who?'

'I dunno, the police or something. Shouldn't you tell your parents?'

'Are you mad? After the fuss they made when they caught me last night?'

'Well,' I say lamely. 'He might do it again. To someone else.'

Claire thinks for a minute. 'No. It must have been me. I got myself into that mess. If I'd just been firmer from the start … '

I look at her, but I don't know what to say. It can't have been her fault, can it? She was dressed – well, she *was* wearing a really short skirt. She wanted the attention, didn't she? But inside my head, I can hear my mum saying, 'Whenever you say no, it means no. Whatever you've said yes to before. No means no.'

'You told him to stop,' I said. 'You were fighting him off. He knew what he was doing was wrong. It's not your fault.'

I can't seem to find the right words, but I know inside that I'm right. It's all so complicated.

'Oh, it doesn't matter now,' sighs Claire. 'We were both drunk. He didn't manage to do anything anyway. I made a mistake. I'll know next time.'

There's a pause as we both stare at the ceiling again.

'So anyway, what about you?' Claire asks finally. 'Did you have a good time at the party?'

I grin. 'I met this boy … '

'Cassie!'

'Nothing happened,' I say. 'Actually, it

was Mark from our class.'

'Mark? The one who sits at the front in Geography?'

'Yeah. He rescued me from some creep in the kitchen who was trying to give me drugs or something.'

Claire's eyes open wide. 'Drugs? To *you*?

I grin. 'I know. I was so freaked out I nearly said yes.'

Claire grabs my arms. 'Who are you? What have you done with Cassie?'

We burst out laughing again. All the hurt from the last week is going away. Where there was a hole inside me, now it's been filled up.

'I was really lonely,' I say to Claire, half-seriously.

'No you weren't,' she says. 'You had *Isabel*.'

I feel a bit uncomfortable. 'She's not like

you, though.'

Claire squeals with laughter. 'Did you *see* her at the party? What did she *look* like!'

'I know. I thought *I* was bad at make-up.'

'No, you looked really nice actually,' Claire nods. 'I liked that top you were wearing.'

My mouth falls open. She obviously doesn't remember that it's the same one I tried on in front of her. 'You said it was a bit revealing last time,' I remind her.

'Last time?' Claire stares back at me. 'I haven't seen it before.'

'Yes, you have. I tried it on when we were in New Look together. You said it wasn't my style.'

'But it looks great on you.'

I open my mouth to argue, but something stops me. This is all so familiar. We've been here before. And I know that if I carry on with it, we'll end up having another row. And I couldn't bear that.

'Never mind.' I shrug. 'It doesn't matter. Fancy going out tomorrow?'

'Down the shopping centre?'

'I dunno,' I say. 'Why don't we go somewhere else for a change?'

Claire looks surprised. 'OK. Where do you want to go?'

'Cinema?' I suggest.

'There's nothing on right now. Let's go bowling.'

I pull a face. 'The squeaky floor makes my ears hurt.'

'Cassie, you're such a wimp.'

'What about swimming?' I ask.

Claire lets out a little scream. 'Are you kidding? Have you *seen* how white I am right now? No one's going to see me in a bikini until I've had my tan done.'

I sigh. Here we go again.

Another great Shades 2.0 title –

by Penny Bates

Here is Chapter One:

ONE

The girl in the thin, summer dress held her hand to her mouth. Her heart beat faster as the huge, dark shapes padded closer and closer. There was a lump in her throat and she could not swallow. She opened her mouth in horror, but the scream would not come. It lay buried deep in her chest, as the two hard-faced boys led the dogs towards her. Now there was nowhere to go. No escape.

'I suppose Sally wants her mum!' The older boy with the bull terrier laughed.

'And such a pity about Sally's pretty, little dress,' the boy with the black Alsatian added. 'Jake'll soon tear that into strips.'

The dogs panted loudly as they pulled on their chains. They sniffed excitedly, as the smell of the girl's sweat reached their noses.

They had followed her from the park. She walked quickly when she sensed them behind her. Then she ran. Another two streets and she would be home. Another two streets and her father would shout and send the boys away. But not this time. The bullies had asked for money when they first spotted Sally on the estate. She told them she didn't have any, because she was only ten. The next day, they pinned her against a wall and searched her pockets.

'She's a skinny kid,' one of the bullies joked, as he threw a pound coin into the air. 'And she'll get even thinner now that we'll be having her dinner money!'

The dogs were a new form of torture. The bull terrier gave short, quick breaths, as the girl struggled to climb the wall at the end of the alley. She could not stop trembling and her legs swung limply beneath her. Then she slid to the ground, like a worn-out rag doll.

'She's just a bag of bones!' one of the boys jeered. 'Food for the dogs.'

'Hardly a meal on her,' the other boy said, as the black Alsatian stared at the child pressed against the wall. 'Jake likes a bit more meat to get his teeth into.'

She begged them to leave her alone, but the dogs started barking and no one could hear. She screamed for her father, but the boys only laughed as they slipped the dogs off their leads. The bull terrier struck first, hurling itself against her legs and knocking her off balance. Then the black dog ran, hot and panting in her face, as she lay on the ground. The black dog thrust its muzzle into her hair and snarled. She felt a trickle of warm saliva run down her cheek. Then the scream tore through her throat, as the dogs fell on top of her. A scream to drown even the snarling and snapping of the dogs.

The man who found her thought she was a piece of rag. Some rubbish thrown against the wall. Then he saw the remains of a child's pretty dress. A rag doll with torn arms held tight against her face. Thin legs were tucked tight into her chest. There had been nowhere to go. Nowhere to hide. She had tried to be invisible, but the dogs would not let go.

'It's over. Everything will be alright,' the man said, as he peeled the girl's hands from her face. Then she heard his sharp intake of breath and knew he was lying.